Under the Sea
A First
Fact Book

ALLSORTED.

First published in 2023 by Allsorted WD19 4BG U.K.

Copyright © Noodle Juice Ltd 2023

Text by Noodle Juice 2022

Illustrations by Liza Lewis 2022

Printed in China

A CIP catalogue record of this book is available from the British Library.

ISBN: 978-1-912295-76-0

1 3 5 7 9 10 8 6 4 2

Contents

4   What is the sea?

6   Under the sea

8   The seashore,
    reefs and mangroves

10 In the depths

12 Frozen oceans

13 Tropical seas

14 Whales

16 Sharks

18 Seals

20 Dolphins

22 Walruses

24 Penguins

26 Lobsters

28 Crabs

30 Octopuses and squid

32 Turtles

34 Eels

36 Seahorses

38 Ocean fish

40 Tropical fish

42 Creatures
    from the deep

44 Jellyfish

46 Anemones
    and urchins

48 Limpets and
    other molluscs

50 Starfish or seastars

52 Can you spot
    them all?

54 Glossary

What is the sea?

Water, in the form of seas and oceans, covers up to 71% of the surface of the Earth. The Pacific Ocean alone takes up almost one third. There are thousands of different species of animal and plant life that live in the water, and many more we haven't even yet discovered.

Fish have lived on Earth for more than 500 million years.

Waves are caused by the wind interacting with the surface of the sea.

There are five oceans that all join up together: Arctic, Atlantic, Indian, Pacific, Southern.

The sea is salty due to the salt and minerals that wash into it from the land.

The water in the sea moves constantly due to the tides and currents.

There are almost 50 seas. Here are some of the more well-known ones:
Adriatic, Aegean, Arabian, Baltic, Black, Caribbean, Caspian, Coral, Dead, Mediterranean, Red.

Under the surface

Fish come in all shapes and sizes. Tiny fish such as plankton are eaten by small fish such as herring, who are in turn eaten by salmon, who get eaten by sharks.

Small fish feel safer in large groups.

Dolphins can swim up to 40 kmph (25 mph) and sometimes follow boats.

The ocean floor is covered in sea urchins, sea anemones and sea sponges. In warmer water, coral reefs provide a home to polyps.

There is plenty of activity under the surface of the ocean. Fish swim in groups called shoals or schools. Dolphins swim in pods. Divers search ancient shipwrecks looking for buried treasure, or survey the seabed looking for signs of oil.

The octopus and the squid are part of the same family as the oyster and the limpet.

The oceans are home to the biggest mammal in the world, the blue whale, but the largest fish is the whale shark.

Seahorses are some of the slowest fish in the ocean. It can take them almost three days to swim 0.8 km (0.5 miles).

Crustaceans such as crabs and lobsters walk across the sea floor.

The seashore, reefs and mangroves

At high tide, the sea comes in to cover the shore, but once the tide has gone out, water is trapped between the rocks to form rock pools.

Rock pools make great hiding places for many sea creatures. Seabirds search for food by turning over pebbles. They are looking for worms, insects or molluscs.

Some crustaceans – animals with a hard shell or skeleton on the outside of their body – bury themselves in the sand.

Sea anemones catch small fish by stinging them with their tentacles.

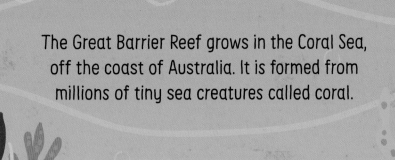

The Great Barrier Reef grows in the Coral Sea, off the coast of Australia. It is formed from millions of tiny sea creatures called coral.

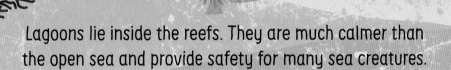

Lagoons lie inside the reefs. They are much calmer than the open sea and provide safety for many sea creatures.

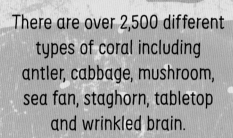

There are over 2,500 different types of coral including antler, cabbage, mushroom, sea fan, staghorn, tabletop and wrinkled brain.

On the Indian coast, trees called mangroves have adapted to the salty conditions and grow wherever there are warm waters.

Mangrove trees have very long roots which help to keep them upright when ocean waves batter them.

In the depths

Some parts of the ocean are very deep indeed. The Mariana Trench, part of the Pacific Ocean, is 11 km (7 miles) below sea level. The deeper you go, the colder and darker the water becomes. Many sea creatures have adapted to their environment to cope with the temperature and lack of light.

These fish all light up!

Some squid can eject a bioluminescent – or light-up – cloud to confuse their enemies.

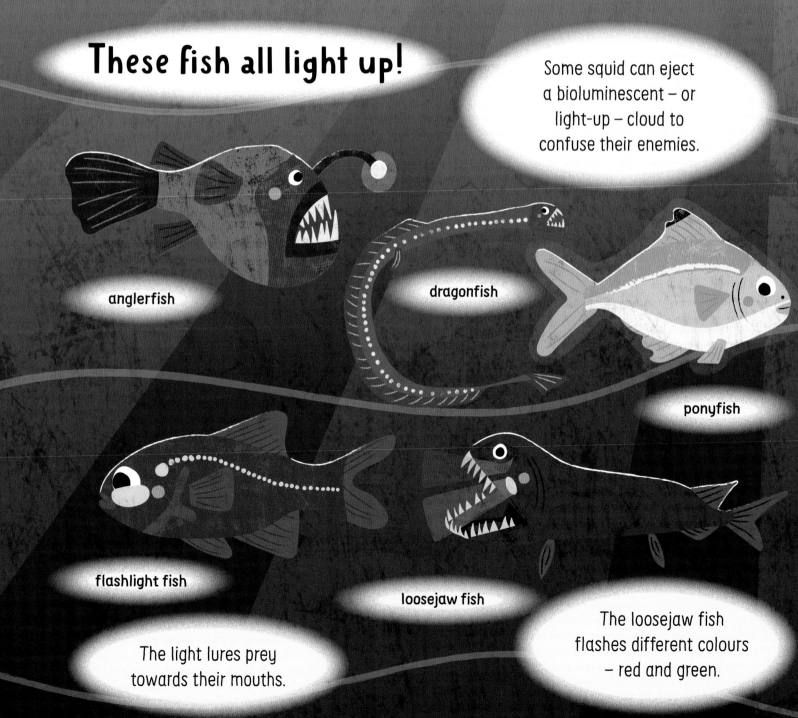

anglerfish

dragonfish

ponyfish

flashlight fish

loosejaw fish

The light lures prey towards their mouths.

The loosejaw fish flashes different colours – red and green.

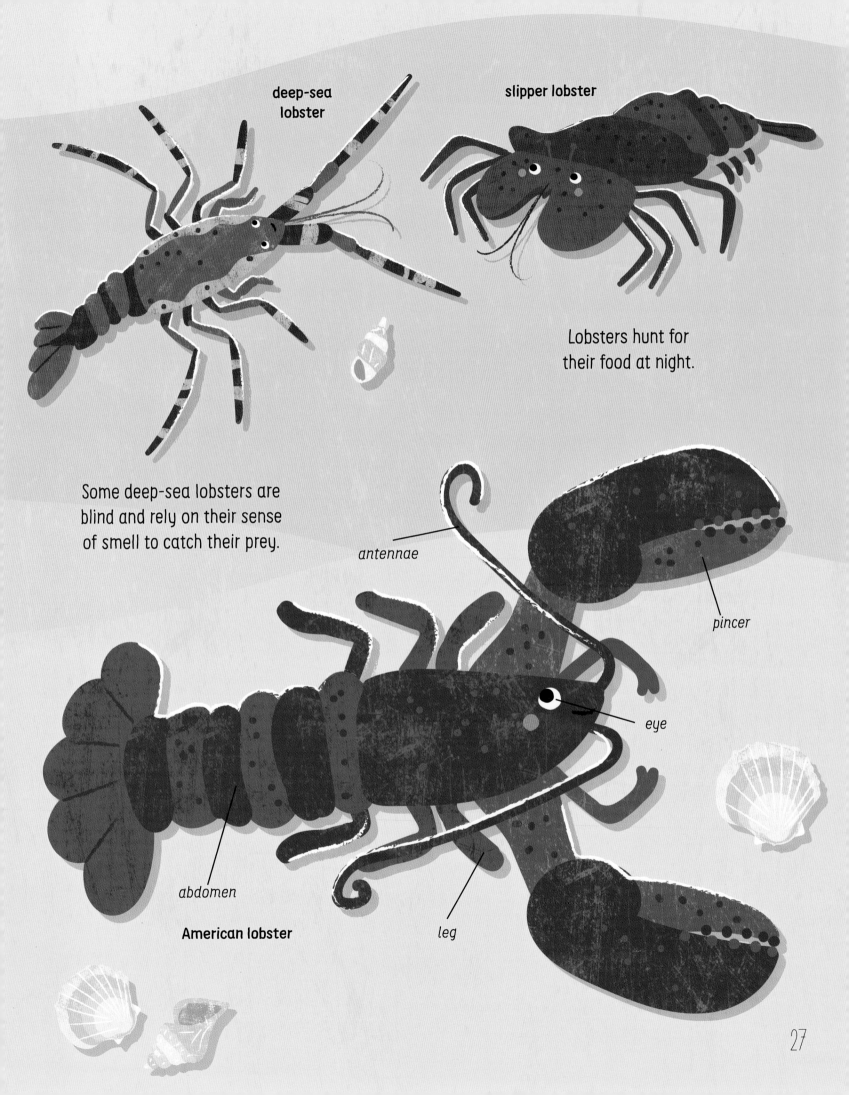

deep-sea lobster

slipper lobster

Lobsters hunt for their food at night.

Some deep-sea lobsters are blind and rely on their sense of smell to catch their prey.

antennae

pincer

eye

abdomen

American lobster

leg

Crabs

Another group of crustaceans, crabs are decapods, meaning that they have ten legs. There are over 10,000 different species of crab.

Crabs are scavengers and help clean up the seabed.

Hermit crabs have softer bodies than other crabs, so they use shells of other creatures to protect themselves.

Crabs, such as the robber crab, migrate to the sea to breed, but now live on land.

common hermit crab

robber crab

Hermit crabs use their first pair of legs as pincers, the next two pairs to walk with and the final two pairs to hold on to its shell.

Some crabs, such as the pea crab, live with other animals. The tiny pea crab lives inside the shells of mussels and oysters.

Most crabs can't swim. They crawl or walk, often sideways, across the ocean floor.

pea crab

blue crab

king crab

edible common crab

Dungeness crab

white-spotted hermit crab

giant crab

Tasmanian crab

yeti crab

spider crab

29

Octopuses and squid

Octopuses and squid both belong to the mollusc family. They have eight arms or legs covered in suckers, and are considered intelligent creatures, due to their large brains.

Most octopuses move by using their limbs to pull them along the ocean floor, although they can shoot backwards by expelling a jet of water.

Female octopuses lay up to 100,000 eggs each time they mate.

dumbo octopus

common octopus

day octopus

The blue-ringed octopus is one of the most poisonous creatures in the world.

The common octopus can change its colour very quickly.

veined octopus

blue-ringed octopus

The octopus's main source of food are crabs and lobsters. Some octopuses eat plankton.

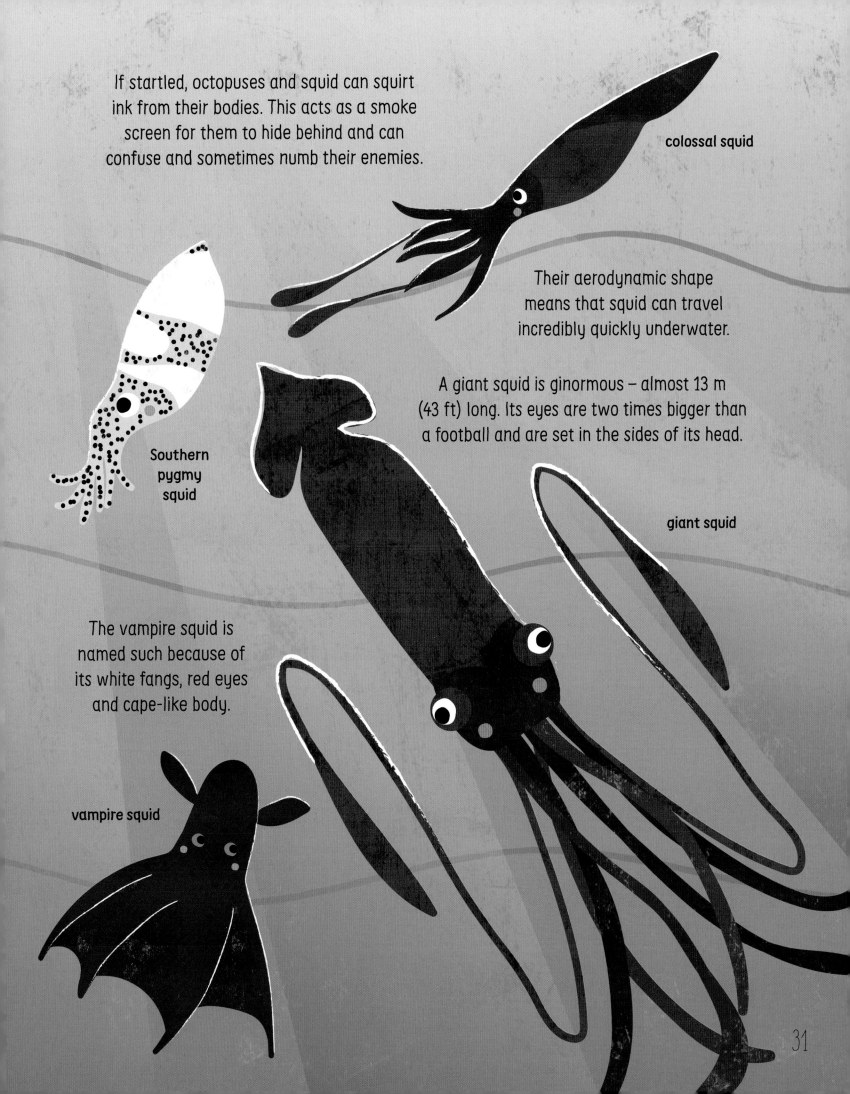

If startled, octopuses and squid can squirt ink from their bodies. This acts as a smoke screen for them to hide behind and can confuse and sometimes numb their enemies.

colossal squid

Their aerodynamic shape means that squid can travel incredibly quickly underwater.

A giant squid is ginormous – almost 13 m (43 ft) long. Its eyes are two times bigger than a football and are set in the sides of its head.

Southern pygmy squid

giant squid

The vampire squid is named such because of its white fangs, red eyes and cape-like body.

vampire squid

31

Turtles

Turtles have been on Earth for over 200 million years, but they haven't changed much in that period. They have a hard shell which they can hide in to protect themselves and very powerful jaws.

Most turtles are meateaters but the green turtle is vegetarian and feeds on algae and seagrasses.

green turtle

flatback turtle

Turtles move quickly through water due to their flipper-like front legs which act as rudders and their back feet which steer.

Some sea-turtle shells can grow as large as 2.4 m (8 ft).

olive ridley turtle

Turtles eat crabs, lobsters and jellyfish.

There are only seven species of sea turtle.

Kemp's ridley turtle

loggerhead turtle

The loggerhead has the largest jaw of all sea turtles, which it uses to crush the shells of whelks and other large molluscs.

leatherback turtle

Leatherback turtles have, as their name suggests, a thick leathery skin instead of the hard scales of other turtles.

hawksbill turtle

Sea turtles lay their eggs on the beach and bury them in the sand. Some swim for hundreds of kilometres to reach their breeding grounds. The olive ridley turtle lays its eggs in mangrove swamps.

Once the eggs hatch, the baby turtles race for the sea before predators can catch them.

Eels

Eels are wormlike fish, some of which, such as the moray eel, live in shallow waters among rocks and reefs. Other eels live in deep seas.

Eels have been around for a very long time – the earliest fossil comes from the Cretaceous period (145.5–65.5 million years ago).

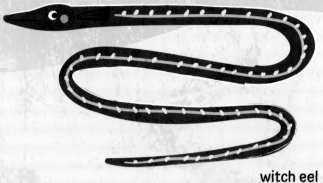

witch eel

sawtooth eel

cutthroat eel

Most eels live on their own and swim slowly by moving in a horizontal S pattern.

snipe eel

All eels migrate in order to breed, but some freshwater eels return to the Sargasso Sea, part of the North Atlantic Ocean, each year.

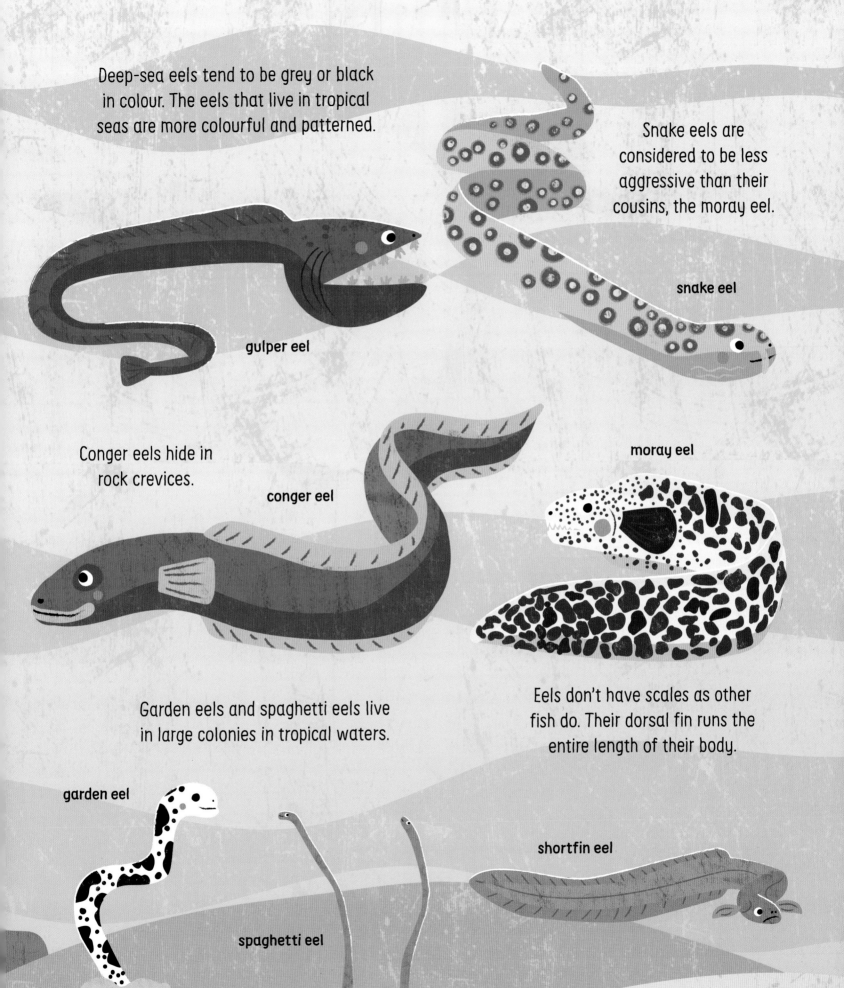

Deep-sea eels tend to be grey or black in colour. The eels that live in tropical seas are more colourful and patterned.

Snake eels are considered to be less aggressive than their cousins, the moray eel.

snake eel

gulper eel

Conger eels hide in rock crevices.

moray eel

conger eel

Garden eels and spaghetti eels live in large colonies in tropical waters.

Eels don't have scales as other fish do. Their dorsal fin runs the entire length of their body.

garden eel

shortfin eel

spaghetti eel

Seahorses

Seahorses move up and down by controlling a tiny pocket of air in their body. They move forwards by fluttering their fins.

The seahorse is the slowest fish in the sea.

Seahorses can range in size from 2–35 cm (0.8–14 inches).

Pacific seahorse

The male seahorse gives birth to seahorse babies after the female seahorse lays her eggs inside a pouch in the male's stomach.

The seahorse can change colour which makes it tricky to spot.

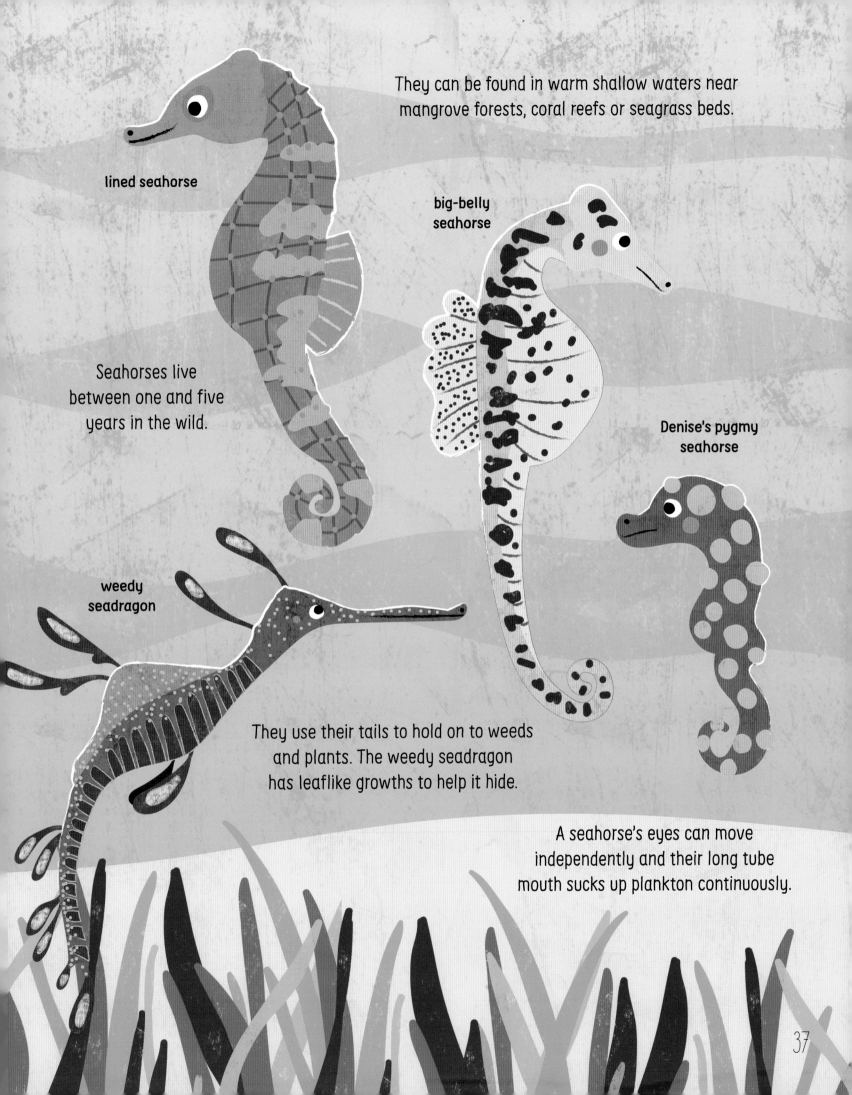

They can be found in warm shallow waters near mangrove forests, coral reefs or seagrass beds.

lined seahorse

big-belly seahorse

Seahorses live between one and five years in the wild.

Denise's pygmy seahorse

weedy seadragon

They use their tails to hold on to weeds and plants. The weedy seadragon has leaflike growths to help it hide.

A seahorse's eyes can move independently and their long tube mouth sucks up plankton continuously.

37

Ocean fish

Most fish breathe through gills and have tastebuds all over their body. They are cold-blooded animals. A lot of fish are covered in scales, and most have fins to help them move through the water.

Smaller fish swim together in shoals, making it hard for predators to pick a single one.

Tuna are large ocean fish. They are unique because they can regulate their body temperature.

tuna

shoal of herring

Plankton-eating fish, like herring and sardines, swim with their mouths open.

Pacific salmon spend most of their lives at sea, but return to the stream where they were born in order to lay their eggs.

sardine

salmon

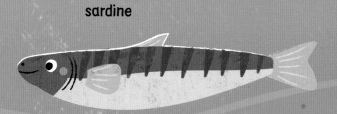

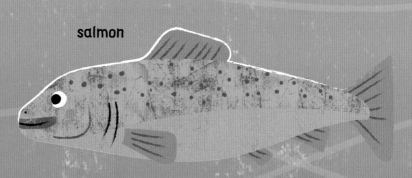

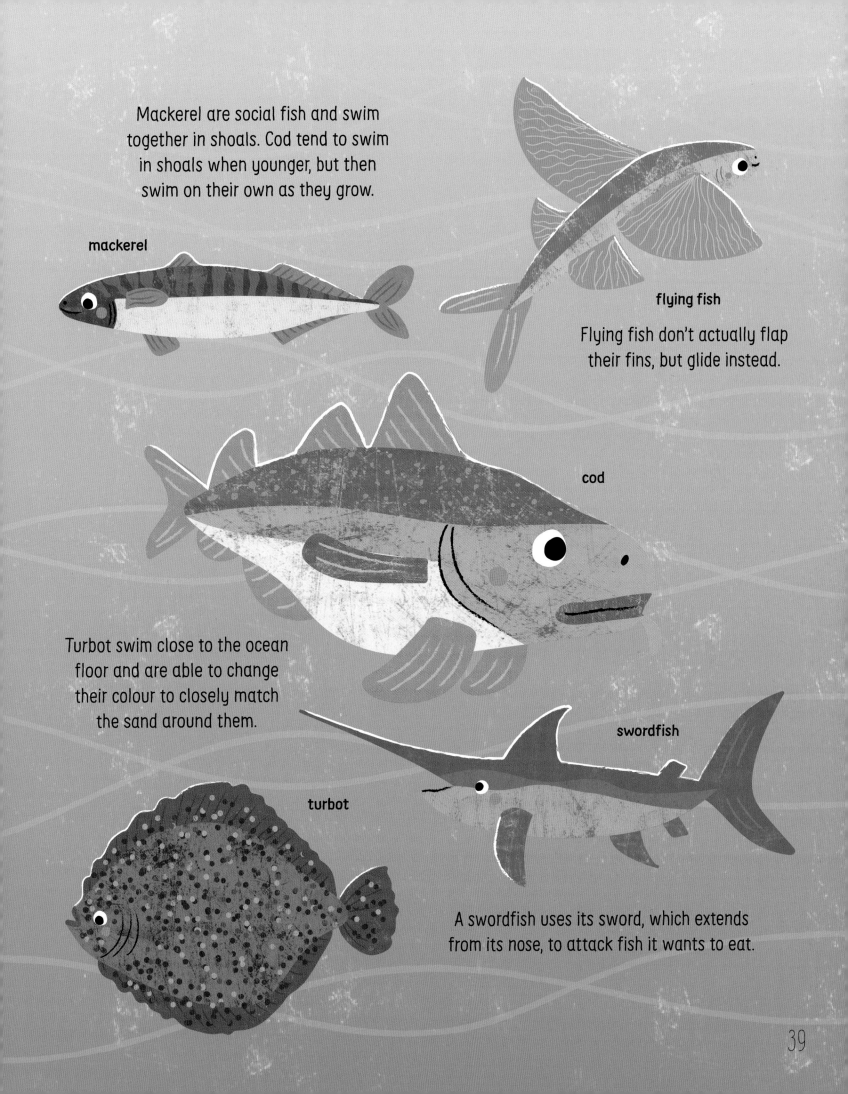

Mackerel are social fish and swim together in shoals. Cod tend to swim in shoals when younger, but then swim on their own as they grow.

mackerel

flying fish

Flying fish don't actually flap their fins, but glide instead.

cod

Turbot swim close to the ocean floor and are able to change their colour to closely match the sand around them.

swordfish

turbot

A swordfish uses its sword, which extends from its nose, to attack fish it wants to eat.

Tropical fish

Fish that swim in tropical waters can be brightly coloured with highly decorative patterns. This colouring is used to attract a mate, or sometimes as protective camouflage.

butterfly fish

yellow tang

royal angelfish

blue tang

mandarin fish

unicorn fish

Lionfish can make their stomachs more than 30 times bigger in order to cope with a large meal.

parrotfish

The parrotfish has grown a beak made from its teeth, so that it can gnaw at coral.

lionfish

When startled, the blowfish swallows lots of water to push out its spines.

clownfish

blowfish

Clownfish avoid danger by hiding in venomous sea anemones. The fish are covered in a slime so they don't get hurt.

Creatures from the deep

Sunlight only penetrates to a certain depth, and beyond that lies the dark abyss where some weird and wonderful sea creatures live.

Fish, such as the loosejaw fish or anglerfish, light up to attract their food or potential mates.

black swallower fish

The black swallower fish is able to stretch its tummy to fit in fish bigger than itself.

anglerfish

wolffish

Tube worms live near deep-sea vents as they depend on the sulphur-munching bacteria surrounding the vents.

tube worms

The wolffish, also known as the catfish, can grow to over 2.3 m (7.5 ft).

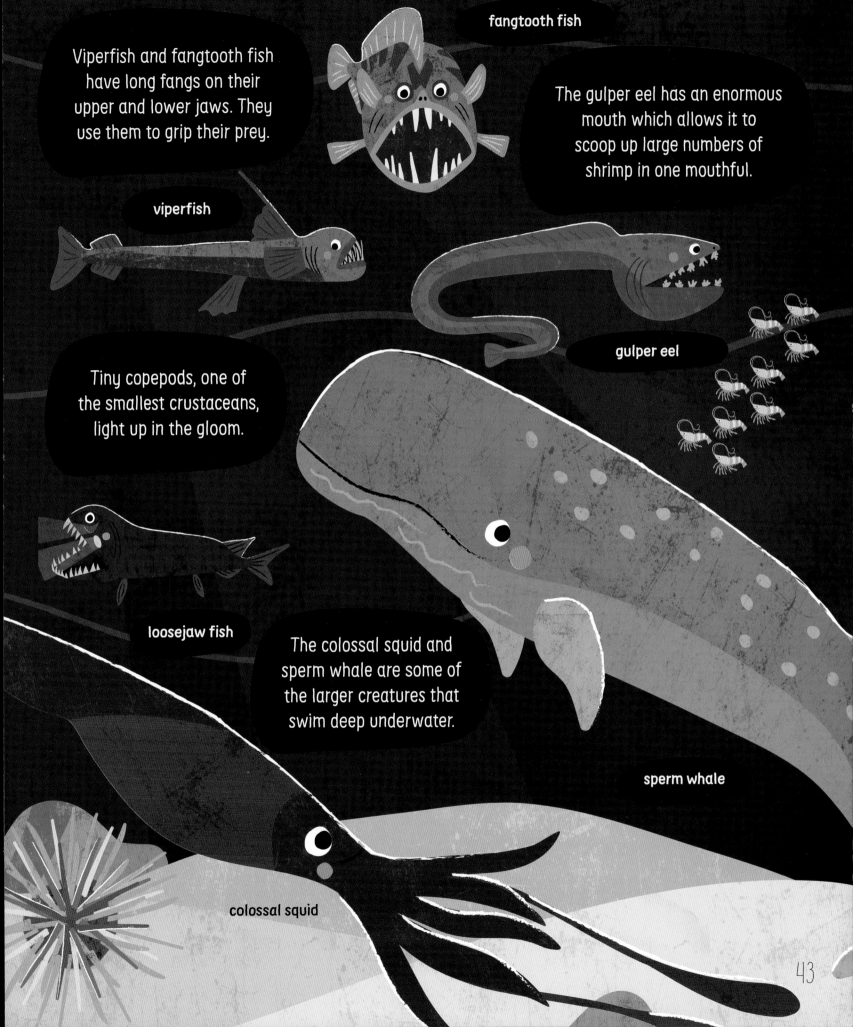

Viperfish and fangtooth fish have long fangs on their upper and lower jaws. They use them to grip their prey.

fangtooth fish

The gulper eel has an enormous mouth which allows it to scoop up large numbers of shrimp in one mouthful.

viperfish

Tiny copepods, one of the smallest crustaceans, light up in the gloom.

gulper eel

loosejaw fish

The colossal squid and sperm whale are some of the larger creatures that swim deep underwater.

sperm whale

colossal squid

Jellyfish

Jellyfish have no brain, no bones or even a heart, and are almost 99% water. Although most jellyfish are harmless, some use their tentacles to sting their prey.

Some jellyfish don't swim. They attach themselves to seaweed or other objects instead.

Free-swimming jellyfish use jet propulsion to move through the water.

football jellyfish

big red jellyfish

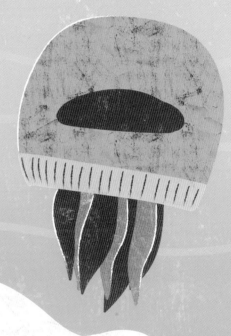

The lion's mane jellyfish is the largest jellyfish in the world. It has up to 150 tentacles and can reach 2.4 m (8 ft) in diameter, and 36.5 m (120 ft) in length.

lion's mane jellyfish

Some jellyfish glow in the dark. Others are almost see-through or transparent, and can be hard to spot in the water.

Jellyfish use the same hole to eat with that they use to poop with.

Cassiopea jellyfish

The Cassiopea jellyfish lives upside down.

sea wasp jellyfish

Portuguese man o'war

box jellyfish

The Portuguese man o'war isn't technically a jellyfish. It is a siphonopore, but is often grouped together with jellyfish due to its bell-shaped body.

Anemones and urchins

These mainly sedentary sea creatures look like underwater flowers, although they can be quite painful if you step on them.

There are over 1,000 different species of sea anemones that live in oceans all over the world.

Normally sea anemones are yellow, blue or green, but some can be bright red or pink.

Some can live in depths of over 10,000 m (33,000 ft).

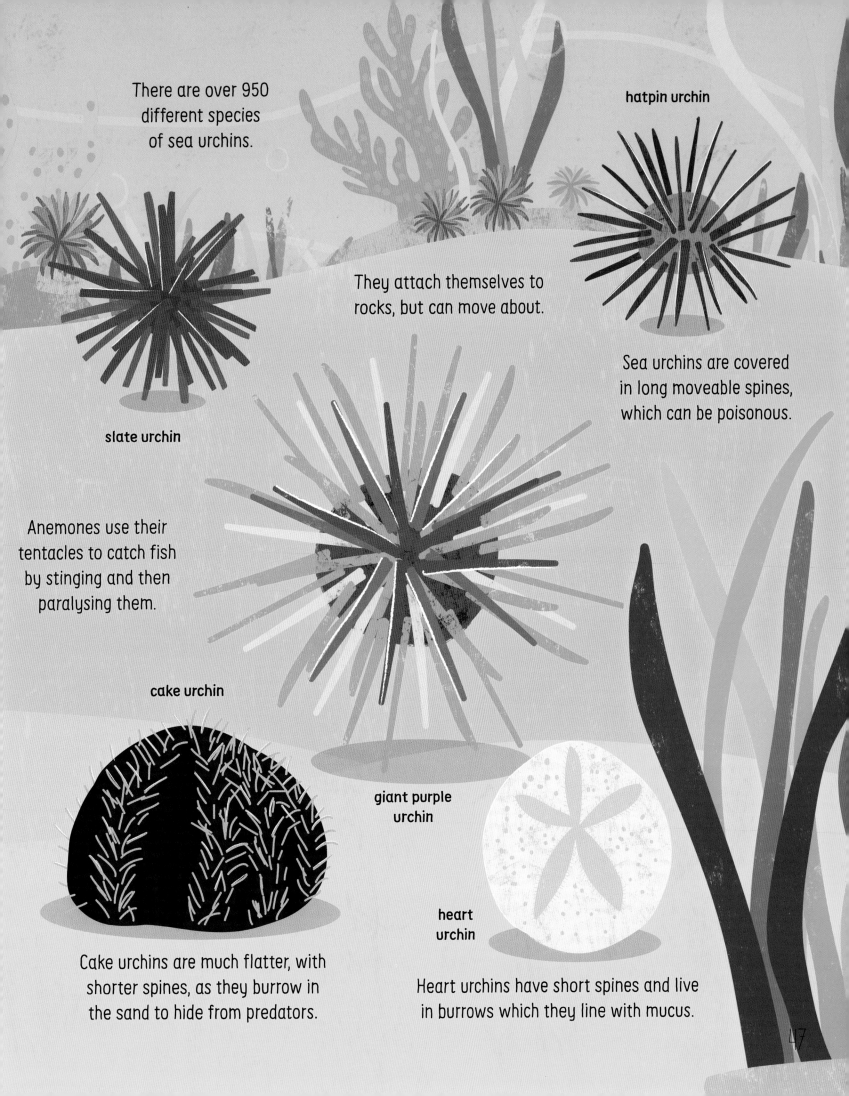

There are over 950 different species of sea urchins.

hatpin urchin

They attach themselves to rocks, but can move about.

Sea urchins are covered in long moveable spines, which can be poisonous.

slate urchin

Anemones use their tentacles to catch fish by stinging and then paralysing them.

cake urchin

giant purple urchin

heart urchin

Cake urchins are much flatter, with shorter spines, as they burrow in the sand to hide from predators.

Heart urchins have short spines and live in burrows which they line with mucus.

47

Limpets and other molluscs

There are many different molluscs in the sea – some have hinged shells such as scallops, others are sea snails, such as whelks.

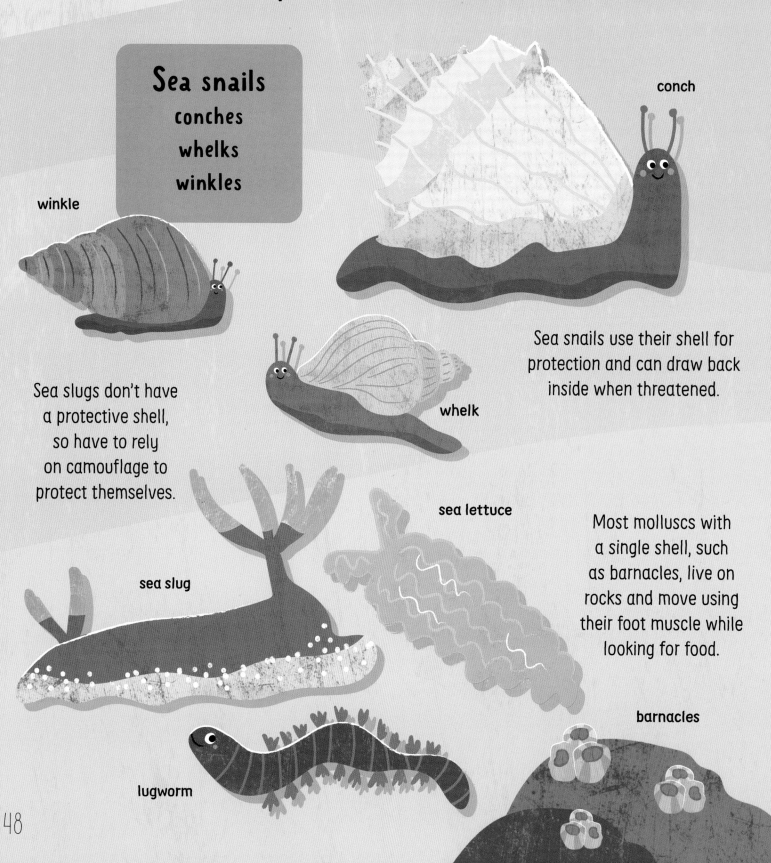

Sea snails
conches
whelks
winkles

winkle

conch

Sea snails use their shell for protection and can draw back inside when threatened.

Sea slugs don't have a protective shell, so have to rely on camouflage to protect themselves.

whelk

sea lettuce

Most molluscs with a single shell, such as barnacles, live on rocks and move using their foot muscle while looking for food.

sea slug

barnacles

lugworm

Hinged shells

clams

mussels

oysters

razor clams

scallops

Two-shelled or bivalve molluscs live on the seabed or in rock pools.

mussels

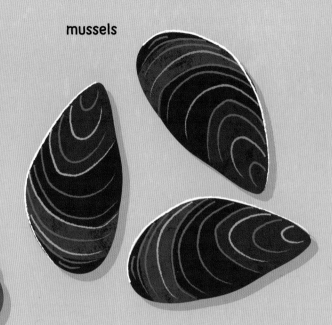

razor clam

Some clams can live for over 100 years, and the giant clam can reach 135 cm (4 ft) in size.

Bivalve molluscs can filter up to 40 litres (10 gallons) of water an hour.

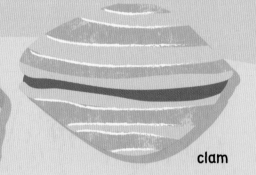

scallops

clam

Some clams use their shells to move through the water by clapping them together.

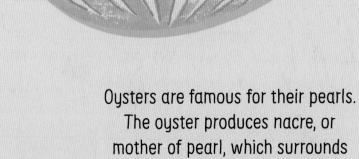

Oysters are famous for their pearls. The oyster produces nacre, or mother of pearl, which surrounds a piece of grit inside the oyster.

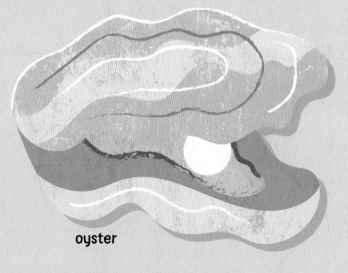

oyster

49